How to be a hero

This book is not like others you have read. This is a ~~ch~~ ny book where Y~~ ~~ dventure.

Each s~~ ~~ is numbered. At the end of most sections, you will have to make a choice. Each choice will take you to a different section of the book.

If you choose correctly, you will succeed. But be careful. If you make a bad choice, you may have to start the adventure again. If this happens, make sure you learn from your mistake!

Go to the next page to start your adventure. And remember, don't be a zero, be a hero!

You are Olympian — a powerful superhero. You were born on Mount Olympus, home of the Greek gods. You are a super-strong runner, jumper and hurdler, and an unbelievable gymnast. You can lift massive weights and can throw your magic javelin, hammer and discus huge distances with amazing accuracy.

You have been sent with your sports trainer, Milo, to protect the good people of River City. You have already helped the police to arrest many crooks, criminal gangs and supervillains, but your greatest challenge is yet to come!

Go to 1.

1

You are on the roof of your secret Sanctuary practising archery. Your target is fixed to the mast of the transmitter tower on Prospect Hill, a kilometre away.

You shoot your last arrow. It lands in the gold centre circle, but Milo — looking through high-powered field glasses — shakes his head. "Eleven arrows in the gold, one in the red. Not good enough, Olympian."

Before you can reply, your wrist communicator flashes red. You are receiving an emergency signal!

"Olympian, this is Detective Keegan of the River City police. We need you down at police HQ straight away. We have reports that there are people all over the city wearing strange metal collars and acting like mindless robots..."

"I bet my old enemy Doctor Robotic is behind this," you say. "I must get to police HQ."

"Be careful," says Milo, "and don't

forget to call on the Flame if you have to."

You nod. If you are in serious danger, you can call upon the Olympic Flame. It will transport you back to the Sanctuary, but it will also rewind time.

"I'll call the police," says Milo. "They'll send a car for you."

If you want to go to police HQ in a police car, go to 18.

If you wish to make your own way there, go to 34.

2

The flying terrobots dive-bomb you. Their eyes flash red and laser bolts shoot towards you. Your Olympian skills are barely enough to dodge their attacks.

As the terrobots continue to attack, more crawlers arrive. They surround you and open their pincers. Once you are in their grasp, there will be no escape!

Go to 23.

3

You find a door leading to a stairway, and head down.

You hear the clanking metal feet of robots on the stairs below. The windows darken as crawler robots scuttle up the outside of the building. They spot you and smash the windows to get in.

You fight well, calling your hammer and discus, as well as the javelin to your aid. But you have little room to use your weapons and there are just too many robots to fight. There is only one way out.

Go to 23.

4

You race through the main doors into the entrance hall of the building and skid to a halt. The hall is full of robots!

You run to the doors but the robots are already firing. A dozen stun-ray beams send you crashing to the floor.

The robots close in. Some of them are holding mind-control collars. They reach towards you.

Go to 23.

5

"How did you get that collar?" you ask the prisoner.

The man doesn't answer. You repeat the question, but again he ignores you.

Suddenly, the door to the room crashes

open. Police officers wearing collars swarm in. A sergeant is carrying another collar. You realise that the other officers are trying to hold you still so that he can fasten it around your neck.

You cannot fight police officers. Your only option is escape.

Go to 23.

6

When you arrive at the tower, you find that it is surrounded by dozens of Doctor Robotic's machines. Terrobots patrol the skies; crawlers, rhinobot tanks and robots swarm around the buildings.

How are you going to get inside the transmitter tower?

If you want to fight your way in, go to 47.

If you want to try to trick your way in, go to 11.

7

You help the guards by pushing away the people with collars on. But the people keep shoving you — even when you force them away again.

You realise that these people are being controlled. It must be the collars! Suddenly the three robots who have the Star Diamond attack you.

If you wish to fight the robots, go to 21.
If you decide to try to snatch the Star Diamond, go to 29.

8

"Javelin!" you cry. "To me!"

You hurl the javelin at the nearest rhinobot, but it simply bounces off the rhinobot's armour. You should have realised that the rhinobots would be much tougher than the terrobots you brought down earlier.

"Time for a new plan," you tell yourself.

Go to 40.

9

You find yourself standing in front of the gleaming robot captain.

"I am Robot Prime," it says. "Where is your mind-control collar?"

You ignore his question. "Are you in charge of all the robots?" you say.

"Yes."

"Then tell me this. Doctor Robotic has started to make humans his mind-slaves. Why do you think he has done that?"

Go to 12.

10

You spot a window up on the wall of the chamber, opening onto a stairway. Your parkour skills enable you to leap up to the window and smash through it. You have escaped from the robots, and now you can get back on Doctor Robotic's trail.

You race up the stairs and reach the roof, only to meet ranks of crawler robots. These swarm towards you, clicking their pincers. A quick glance shows you that others are swarming up the outside of the building.

If you decide to fight the crawlers, go to 27.

If you want to avoid them, go to 37.

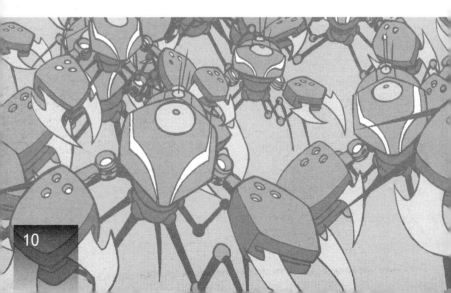

11

You decide to try to trick your way in. As a mind-slave shuffles past, you step out from your hiding place and put your hands up. The mind-slave sees that you don't have a collar and shoves you towards the transmitter tower. He's taking you inside.

Go to 22.

12

The robot's electronic eyes stare at you. "Explain."

"Robots are expensive," you say. "Humans are cheap. With his mind-control collars, Doctor Robotic can create an army of mind-slaves. Then he will not need robots."

Robot Prime nods. "That is logical. Come with me. We will hear what Doctor Robotic has to say."

To go with Robot Prime, go to 24.
If you decide to attack it, go to 38.

13

You enter police HQ. You stare around in horror. Every police officer is wearing a control collar!

They grab you and try to fasten a collar around your neck. You cannot fight them, they don't know what they are doing. There is only one way out.

Go to 23.

14

This is your last chance.

You hurl yourself at Doctor Robotic and run up the front of his suit, treating the exoskeleton like an obstacle in parkour. As you backflip away, Doctor Robotic fires his cannon at you — but you've already moved! Instead of hitting you, the cannon-shell blasts the suit's power-source.

The exoskeleton topples over with Doctor Robotic trapped inside. His control is broken. All the robots stop moving. The mind-slaves blink and look around them.

You fold your arms and gaze at Doctor Robotic as he struggles to get out of the ruined suit. "Doctor Robotic, you're under arrest for crimes against River City — and for giving me a really hard day."

Go to 50.

15

Using your parkour skills, you climb onto the roof. You find an unguarded doorway and steps that lead down.

You sneak through the corridors, dodging robots and people wearing collars.

You are in an empty corridor when a squad of robots appears. Not wanting to attract their attention, you slip into a room marked "Mailroom".

Inside, robots are busy unpacking and handing out mind-control collars.

To destroy the collars, go to 41.

If you think you should find out who is controlling the robots, go to 20.

16

You leap from rooftop to rooftop. When you are clear of City Hall, you jump down and pause to think.

You realise that your escape has brought you near the transmitter tower on Prospect Hill. It still has your archery target fixed to the mast that beams TV, radio and mobile phone signals to the whole city.

You are thunderstruck. Why hadn't you thought of it before? This is the obvious place for Doctor Robotic to send the signals controlling his mind-slave collars!

As you head for the transmitter tower, two of Doctor Robotic's rhinobot tanks trundle around a corner. You have to make a quick decision!

To use your javelin against the rhinobot tanks, go to 8.

To use your strength, go to 40.

17

You decide to go down fighting. You send your discus skimming towards another robot, but the rest move back to use their stun-ray beams. Bolts of energy blast you, leaving you weak and helpless.

The robots close in. Several are holding mind-control collars.

Go to 23.

18

A police car pulls up just as you reach the kerb. You get in. "Police HQ," you tell the driver.

As the car moves off, siren blaring, you realise the driver is wearing a metal collar. His eyes in the rear-view mirror are blank and staring.

"Let me out!" You reach for the door handle.

The driver presses a button. Green gas floods your half of the car.

Go to 23.

19

You dodge behind robot after robot. As he tries to hit you, Doctor Robotic blasts more and more of his machines.

But despite your speed, you cannot run faster than a cannon shell. One explodes nearby, knocking you off your feet.

Robots drag you back to face Doctor Robotic.

He raises his cannon to blast you. With the last of your strength, you break free from the robots.

If you want to fight on, go to 28.
If you want to try to get behind Doctor Robotic, go to 48.

You find the council chamber and slip inside.

The mayor is tied up in his official seat, guarded by robots. Next to him stands a strange figure: half man, half robot. He reaches into a box of mind-control collars and takes one out.

"Just as I thought," you mutter. "Doctor Robotic!"

The mayor struggles against his bonds.

Doctor Robotic reaches out to fasten the collar around the mayor's neck. "These collars will turn River City into Mind-slave City!"

If you want to help the mayor, go to 45.
To wait and see what happens, go to 32.

21

"Hammer! To me!" you cry.

Instantly, the hand-held wrecking ball used in the Olympic hammer-throw is in your hands.

A steel ball weighing more than seven kilograms at the end of a chain 120 centimetres long is an ideal tool for smashing robots! You launch yourself into a spin and send metal body parts flying.

Now there are only two robots. One moves towards you, while the last one runs off down the street. It must have the diamond!

If you want to fight the robot, go to 46.
If you want to get away and follow the robot with the diamond, turn to 43.

22

With the mind-slave pushing you forwards, you walk right past the robots defending the transmitter tower. Your trick seems to be working. You spot a robot that is bigger and better built than the others. You hear it giving orders to the other robots, which salute it. This robot can speak! You guess that it must be the robot captain.

If you wish to attack the robot captain, go to 42.

If you want to speak to it, go to 9.

23

"Flame! To me!" you cry.

The Olympic Flame forms around you in a swirl of light. When the flame dies, you are back in the Sanctuary.

You explain to Milo why you had to call on the Flame to save you.

Milo is angry. "You've had a lucky escape," he growls. "Didn't I tell you to be always on your guard?"

You know your trainer is right. You have been careless. You will have to start your quest to save River City again.

Go to 49.

24

As Robot Prime beckons you to follow, Doctor Robotic appears. He is wearing a powerful exoskeleton.

Robot Prime steps forward. "This human says you will replace robots with mind-slaves."

Doctor Robotic glares at you. "You have interfered with my plans for the last time, Olympian!"

He raises his arm cannon and aims it straight at you.

If you want to dodge behind Robot Prime, go to 44.

If you decide to ask Robot Prime to save you, go to 31.

25

Your parkour skills take you swiftly through the city streets. Soon you spot a robot carrying pizza boxes.

"Interesting," you mutter to yourself. "Robots don't eat pizza — but Doctor Robotic does..."

Go to 43.

26

You race after Doctor Robotic.

"Robots!" he cries. "Mind-slaves! Protect me!"

By the time you have fought your way clear, Doctor Robotic is far ahead. You follow him out of the building and see him climbing into a rhinobot tank, which heads straight for you. Behind him is an entire robot army!

If you wish to call on the Olympic Flame to save you, go to 23.

If you want to leap up onto the rooftop to escape, go to 16.

27

"Hammer!" you cry. "To me!"

Soon you are smashing the robots to pieces. But what the crawlers lack in strength, they make up for in agility. One seizes you by the ankle. A terrific shock surges through your body. Too late, you realise that each of the crawlers' pincers contains an electric stun-ray.

Go to 23.

28

Doctor Robotic fires. You jump out of the way of the shell, which explodes harmlessly to one side.

Doctor Robotic is furious. "Stand still!" he snarls.

But you now know you can move faster than Doctor Robotic can aim and fire.

If you want to run for your life, go to 36.

If you want to make one last attempt to defeat Doctor Robotic, go to 14.

29

You leap over the three robots, snatching the diamond from them.

In seconds, you are on a rooftop with the Star Diamond safely in your belt-pouch. The people wearing collars just stand and stare up at you. Two of the robots try to climb after you. They fall and smash as they hit the ground. The last robot walks off down the street away from the mind-slaves.

If you want to follow the robot, go to 43.

If you wish to take the Star Diamond to the police, go to 13.

30

"Javelin! To me!" you cry.

Your javelin appears in your hand. You throw it at the first terrobot. Its point rips through the flying robot. Then it curves round to hit the others.

More terrobots appear in the distance. They haven't spotted you yet, but your position on the rooftop is dangerous.

If you want to take shelter inside the building, go to 3.

To escape over the rooftops, go to 16.

31

If a shell from Doctor Robotic's cannon hits you, you will be toast!

You turn to Robot Prime. "Stop him!"

"I cannot," says the robot. "He is my master. I must obey his orders."

Doctor Robotic laughs.

If you want to run for your life, go to 36.

To hide behind Robot Prime, go to 44.

32

Doctor Robotic fastens the collar around the mayor's neck. "Now you will do anything I tell you!" he laughs.

You decide to steal a collar to find out how it works. But as you step out of hiding, Doctor Robotic spots you. He laughs. "Olympian!"

You point an accusing finger. "Doctor Robotic! You're under arrest!"

"For what?" he scoffs. "Stealing a diamond? My mind-slaves will do anything I want!" He points at you. "Attack!"

He runs for the door as his robots lumber forward.

If you want to fight the robots, go to 35.
If you want to try to escape, go to 10.

33

"I have important information," you tell your robot captors.

One of them brings out a mind-control collar.

"If you make me a mind-slave," you say quickly, "Doctor Robotic will never find out what I know."

This time, the robots seem to understand you. One of them leads you inside the transmitter tower, where there are more robots. You are taken towards the large robot captain.

To attack the robot captain, go to 42.
To speak to the robot captain, go to 9.

34

"Don't bother!" you tell Milo. "Going by car will cramp my style. I can travel faster using my parkour skills."

You speed across the city, leaping up walls and across rooftops.

Go to 49.

35

"Hammer! To me!" you cry.

The hammer appears in your hands. You use it to smash your way through the robots, but more pour into the council chamber. Doctor Robotic is escaping!

If you wish to call on the Olympic Flame to save you, go to 23.

To look for another way out, go to 10.

36

You turn and run.

Doctor Robotic laughs. "Coward! My robots will deal with you."

Crawlers and robots stream after you. Ahead is a line of rhinobot tanks. Terrobots swoop down to attack. There is only one way to escape.

Go to 23.

37

You leap onto the next roof to escape the crawler robots.

Two of the crawlers try to follow, but they can't jump as far, and crash down on the street. You wave to the others. "So long, creeps!"

A high-pitched whine causes you to spin around fast. Speeding out of the sky towards you are flying robots.

You groan. "Terrobots!"

If you want to try to outrun the terrobots, go to 2.

If you want to attack them with your javelin, go to 30.

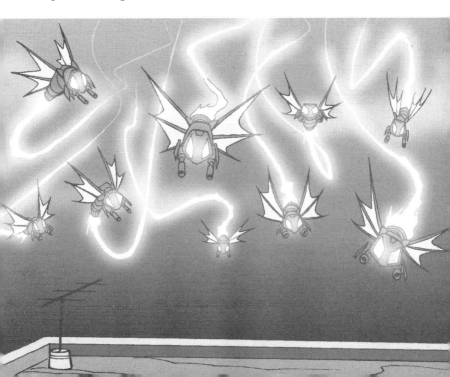

38

"Discus, to me!" you cry.

The discus appears in your hand and you skim it at Robot Prime. However, the robot dodges the discus and spins around and grabs you. "You are a liar," it says, and blasts you with a stun-ray.

Go to 23.

39

Your free-running skills quickly take you to the museum.

The museum guards are struggling with humans who are wearing the strange metal collars. Three powerful robots have the Star Diamond.

If you want to help the guards, go to 7.

If you want to attack the robots, go to 21.

If you want to try to snatch the diamond, go to 29.

40

The nearest rhinobot charges.

Instead of trying to jump over it, you slide underneath. "Up you come!"

You pick the rhinobot off the ground. You hurl the robot tank, crashing it into the other rhinobot.

You head for the transmitter tower.

Go to 6.

41

"Discus! To me!" you cry.

Instantly your Olympian discus appears in your hand. You skim it around the room, smashing several collars and disabling two robots. The rest hide under tables.

But you soon realise that there are too many collars for you to destroy this way. While these robots are distracted, you should find out who is controlling them. You slip away.

Go to 20.

42

You stride towards the robot captain — if you can disable it, perhaps the other robots will stop working. "Discus! To me!" you cry.

Before you can throw your discus, the robot captain turns on you. "You don't have a collar!" It calls to the other robots. "Attack!"

The robots fire. Their stun-ray beams send you crashing to the ground. The discus falls from your hand.

Robots holding mind-control collars reach towards you.

Go to 23.

43

You follow the robot. It heads to City Hall.

"Perhaps whoever is controlling the robots and the people wearing collars," you mutter to yourself, "is in there."

If you want to follow the robot through the main entrance of City Hall, go to 4.

To find another way in, go to 15.

You take cover behind Robot Prime as Doctor Robotic fires. The cannon shells hit the robot.

Robot Prime staggers under the impact. Sparks burst from its metal body. It stares up at Doctor Robotic. "You have betrayed us!" Then it clatters to the ground.

Doctor Robotic is furious. "You will pay for that, Olympian!" He takes aim again.

If you want to try to dodge Doctor Robotic's shot, go to 19.

If you want to try to get behind Doctor Robotic, go to 48.

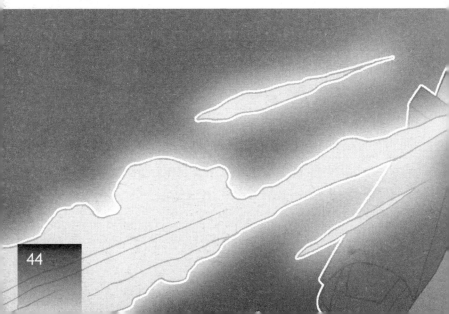

45

"Javelin! To me!" you whisper.

Instantly, your javelin appears in your hand. You throw it and knock the mind-control collar out of Doctor Robotic's hand. It breaks with a shower of sparks.

Doctor Robotic spins around and spots you. "Olympian!" he snarls. "Robots! Seize him!"

The robots lumber towards you, while Doctor Robotic runs for the door.

To follow Doctor Robotic, go to 26.
If you decide to fight the robots, go to 35.

46

Hammer flailing, you smash the last robot.

However, you immediately realise that you have no idea who sent the robots or where they came from.

If you wish to find more robots to follow, go to 25.

If you decide to go back to police HQ for more information, go to 13.

47

"Discus! Javelin! To me!" you cry.

You skim your discus at the robot warrriors. You knock several down. While the discus is still in the air, your javelin takes out a dozen terrobots.

You vault over the rhinobot tanks. You are nearly at the transmitter tower!

But the other robots attack again. One grabs your arm. There are just too many robots!

If you want to continue the attack, go to 17.

If you decide to let yourself be captured, go to 33.

48

As Doctor Robotic takes aim, you slide between the exoskeleton's legs and leap onto its shoulders. Doctor Robotic can't reach you here with his weapons.

"Get this pest off me!" he orders his robots.

Robot Prime lifts its head. "No!" it rasps. "Doctor Robotic has lied to us. Do not harm the human."

As the robots hesitate, you realise that the power for Doctor Robotic's exoskeleton is carried along cables. You reach around the shoulder and rip away two of the cables. The suit's left arm stops working.

But Doctor Robotic reaches across with his cannon arm and swats you from his shoulder, knocking you to the ground.

He raises his cannon. "Goodbye, Olympian!"

If you want to run for your life, go to 36.

If you want to make one last attempt to defeat Doctor Robotic, go to 14.

49

You go to police HQ where Detective Keegan shows you a man wearing a metal collar. He has a blank expression.

"He won't answer questions," says Keegan. "He doesn't seem to hear them. It's like something in that collar is controlling his mind."

You reach out to take off the collar.

"Don't!" says Keegan sharply. "We tried that. The collars give a lethal electric shock if anyone tries to tamper with them."

Keegan's radio bursts into life. "Report to River City Museum. The Star Diamond is being stolen!"

Keegan clenches her fists. "That's the most valuable diamond in the world!" She runs from the room.

If you want to question the man in the collar, go to 5.

If you decide to head for the museum, go to 39.

When Detective Keegan arrives with Milo and the mayor, Doctor Robotic is still struggling to get out of his smashed exoskeleton.

"You'd better call police HQ," you tell Detective Keegan, "and ask them to send a prison van — and a can opener."

Milo nods his head. "Good enough, Olympian."

"I thought Doctor Robotic had us licked this time," says Keegan. "How did you beat him?"

You grin. "You could say he shot himself in the foot."

The mayor holds out his hand. "However you did it, you've saved River City. You are a hero!"

Immortals

HERO

I HERO Quiz

Test yourself with this special quiz. It has been designed to see how much you remember about the book you've just read. Can you get all five answers right?

To download the answer sheets simply visit:

www.hachettechildrens.co.uk

Enter the "Teacher Zone" and search "Immortals".

Question 1

What is the name of the robot captain?

A   Robot Prime

B   Robot Alpha

C   Doctor Robotic

D   Milo

Question 2

What does Doctor Robotic do when you are taken to see him at the transmitter tower?

A   he turns you into a robot

B   he raises his arm cannon

C   he runs away

D   he puts you in prison

Question 3

What is the name of the police detective?

A   Detective Logan

B   Detective Keegan

C   Detective Kellar

D   Detective Kelly

Question 4

How do you defeat Doctor Robotic?

A   the transmitter tower blows up

B   you throw a discus at him

C   he shoots himself

D   his robots jump on him

Question 5

How do you destroy the terrobots when you are on the rooftop in River City?

A   you throw your hammer

B   you ask for Milo's help

C   you call on the Olympic Flame

D   you throw your javelin

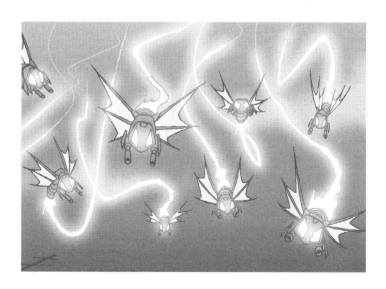

About the 2Steves

"The 2Steves" are Britain's most popular writing double act for young people, specialising in comedy and adventure. They perform regularly in schools and libraries, and at festivals, taking the power of words and story to audiences of all ages.

Together they have written many books, including the *Crime Team* series.
Find out what they've been up to at:
www.the2steves.net

About the illustrator: Jack Lawrence

Jack Lawrence is a successful freelance comics illustrator, working on titles such as *A.T.O.M.*, Cartoon Network, *Doctor Who Adventures*, *2000 AD*, *Gogos Mega Metropolis* and *Spider-Man Tower of Power*. He also works as a freelance toy designer.

Jack lives in Maidstone in Kent with his partner and two cats.

Have you completed the I HERO Quests?

Battle with aliens in Tyranno Quest:

978 1 4451 0875 9 pb
978 1 4451 1345 6 ebook

978 1 4451 0876 6 pb
978 1 4451 1346 3 ebook

978 1 4451 0877 3 pb
978 1 4451 1347 0 ebook

978 1 4451 0878 0 pb
978 1 4451 1348 7 ebook

Defeat the Red Queen in Blood Crown Quest:

978 1 4451 1499 6 pb
978 1 4451 1503 0 ebook

978 1 4451 1500 9 pb
978 1 4451 1504 7 ebook

978 1 4451 1501 6 pb
978 1 4451 1505 4 ebook

978 1 4451 1502 3 pb
978 1 4451 1506 1 ebook

Save planet Earth in Atlantis Quest:

978 1 4451 2867 2 pb
978 1 4451 2868 9 ebook

978 1 4451 2870 2 pb
978 1 4451 2871 9 ebook

978 1 4451 2876 4 pb
978 1 4451 2877 1 ebook

978 1 4451 2873 3 pb
978 1 4451 2874 0 ebook

Also by the 2Steves...

978 0 7496 9283 4 pb
978 1 4451 0843 8 eBook

A millionaire is found at his luxury
island home – dead! But no one can
work out how he died. You must get
to Skull Island and solve the mystery
before his killer escapes.

978 0 7496 9284 1 pb
978 1 4451 0844 5 eBook

The daughter of a Hong Kong
businessman has been kidnapped.
You must find her, but who took
her and why? You must crack the
case, before it's too late!

978 0 7496 9286 5 pb
978 1 4451 0845 2 eBook

You must solve the clues to stop
a terrorist attack in London.
But who is planning the attack,
and when will it take place? It's
a race against time!

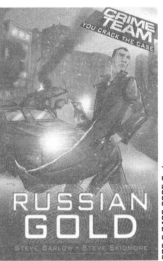

978 0 7496 9285 8 pb
978 1 4451 0846 9 eBook

An armoured convoy has been
attacked in Moscow and hundreds
of gold bars stolen. But who was
behind the raid, and where is the
gold? Get the clues – get the gold.